Story by
Rhoda Levine
Pictures by Edward Gorey

HE WAS THERE FROM THE DAY WE MOVED IN

A Harlin Quist Book

DEDICATED TO GEORGE X. LEVINE WITH LOVE
PUBLISHED BY HARLAN QUIST, INC.
DISTRIBUTED BY DIAL/DELACORTE SALES
1 DAG HAMMARSKJOLD PLAZA, NEW YORK 10017
TEXT COPYRIGHT © 1968 BY RHODA LEVINE
PICTURES COPYRIGHT © 1968 BY EDWARD GOREY
ALL RIGHTS RESERVED
LIBRARY OF CONGRESS CARD: 68-18197
ISBN PAPERBACK: 0-8252-3522-7
ISBN HARDCOVER: 0-8252-3524-3
FOURTH PRINTING
PRINTED IN THE U.S.A.
DESIGNED BY PATRICK COURATIN

He was there from the day we moved in. He was there sitting in the garden.

"I wonder if he comes with the yard?" my brother Ogden asked, as we looked through the window.

"No one mentioned him when we bought th
house," my father replied in a puzzled voice. "
wonder what he wants?"

"I think he is waiting for something," I said

He certainly did look like he was waiting fo
something, we all agreed.

He is waiting for *me-e-e!*" my brother Ogden
shouted suddenly, running through the kitchen
into the back yard.

My brother Ogden is four.

"I'm sure he is waiting for all of us," my mother
insisted, as we followed in Ogden's footsteps.

We stood there in front of him. He seemed neither pleased nor disappointed to see us.

"Maybe he is waiting for me to jump up and down," my brother Ogden suggested, jumping up and down.

"Maybe he wants me to do a somersault!" Ogden had just learned to somersault.

"I know!" breathlessly Ogden guessed again. "He wants to see me skip on two feet!"

"I think," said my mother, placing a quieting and comforting hand on Ogden, "he is waiting for something to eat." My mother is a very practical woman.

, myself, did not feel that that was the answer. But watched my mother bring a bowl of milk, a raw amburger and a soup bone, which she put down 1 front of him. Ogden ran to get a sticky lollypop. t was green! But, after all, Ogden is only four.

Well, he looked at everything. He gave every-hing a try – except, of course, the lollypop. I hate reen myself.

"He's waiting again! . . . He's waiting for some thing else! . . . What's he waiting for?" Ogden wa pretty troubled.

"I am sure he is waiting to get to know us," m mother said as she led us indoors. "He just need to think about us overnight."

Well, that night I certainly thought a lot abou him. Of course, I didn't do anything silly like run ning to the window in my bare feet, to see if he wa still there! Ogden did that.

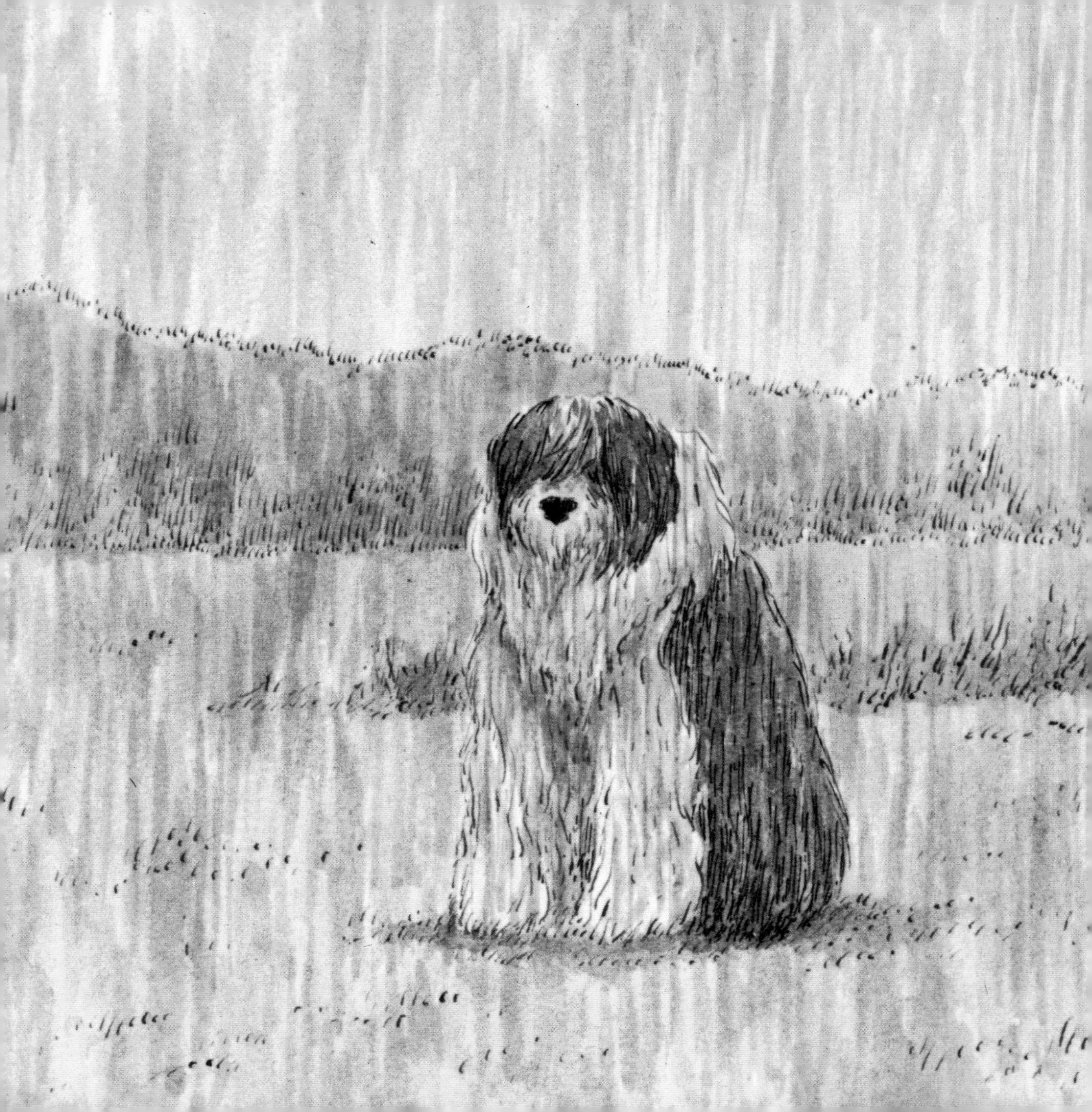

He was there the next morning. It was raining, but
e didn't seem to notice.

My mother smiled. "I'm sure he is waiting to be
nvited in," she decided. She can never stand to see
nyone sitting in the rain.

Well, right away, Ogden ran out to him. "My
nother says c'mon in the house, so c'mon, c'mon!"
Nothing happened, so Ogden ran a line of corn
lakes from the door to the dog. "C'mon, please,"
e added, quietly.

But he just sat there, his fur dripping, waiting . . .

The days passed. We fed him. When it got cool, w
covered him with a blanket. He didn't seem t
mind. While, all the time, Ogden tried harder an
harder to find out what he was waiting for.

Once Ogden thought he might want a piece c
string.

He tried to bring him a stray cat.

He even tried a box of crayons

. . . and a calendar.

Ogden thought he might want to be "talked to. Do you know, my brother spent a whole afternoo just sitting and talking to him! A whole afternoo is a pretty long time!

Ogden told me once that he was *sure* he was waiting
for a new toy truck.

I really thought that Ogden was waiting for
that himself.

When nothing worked, Ogden began to calm down.
Sometimes he didn't talk about him or visit him at
all! . . . Well, it's hard to stay interested in some
one who is not interested in you, I don't care how
old you are!

, however, never forgot about him and what he
might be waiting for. I never stopped thinking
about it – not even when I was asleep, not even
when I was playing ball, not even when I was
reading.

Well, one night, I guess I was thinking harder than usual. I had been studying him as he sat in the moonlight with his eyes closed. "Listen," I thought, "you've got food, friends, a home. What is it you *really* want?"

Well, suddenly, I knew, just like that!

He wanted a name! *He was waiting for a name!*

The next morning I started a list. I wrote dow
every name I had ever heard. I looked for names i
all the books we owned. I even looked on truck
and posters! Not that I intended to call hin
MATT'S MACHINE SHOP or ACME WRECK
ING or anything like that. I just wanted to get uj
a good store of possibilities.

Naming a grownup dog is not like naming
baby, you know. You have to find the exact on
that suits him, the one that he has been waiting for
You can't jump into a name just like that!

By dinner time, I had the longest list I had ever seen – and very interesting too – with the best names traced over in fountain pen.

"What are you drawing?" Ogden asked. My brother Ogden can't read.

"I'm not drawing," I said. "I'm writing."

"What are you writing?"

That's when I made my big mistake. I told Ogden what I was writing, and why. Ogden's eyes grew wide when I told him. Sometimes he thinks I am pretty smart. His eyes got so wide that I didn't notice he was backing up while I talked.

Suddenly he was gone! He was running toward the back yard yelling, "I know, *I know his name!*" He was in the yard before I could stop him. Sometimes four year olds can run faster than anyone.

"Wait," I cried, "you've got to think before–" But I guess he just couldn't stop. I was sort of glad my parents were doing the dishes so they didn't have to see what happened.

Ogden ran right up to him, stopped short and pointed at his nose. "Your name!" Ogden was breathless. "Your name! *I know your name!* It's –" He lifted up an ear and whispered into it. Then he stepped back. I have never seen Ogden look so proud and happy!

We didn't breathe for a whole minute. That dog just blinked. Then, slowly, he looked up with sad and patient eyes. He blinked again, like he wa giving it a second thought. Then he stood up, shool himself, and began to walk – like he was old and tired – toward the end of the garden.

Well, when Ogden told me the name he whisper ed, I must say that I would have walked away too Well, whoever heard of naming a dog *Marilyn* even if it is the name of the girl who used to liv next door!

I thought Ogden was pretty dumb, but I didn' tell him. He looked so sad standing there. I mear *really* sad!

I guess it was the way that Ogden looked that mad
me do it. Suddenly I took off after that dog. I go
right in front of him and started talking.

He kept padding along . . .

"Listen," I said, "I've got a list of possible name
you haven't heard yet! Names like Bouncer
Arthur, George and Garson –"

He kept walking. He blinked.

"Oh, I know they may not be the right names,"
added quickly, "but I've got others. French names
names of places, adjectives and everything. Well
you've just got to give me a chance!"

He shook himself.

"Listen, my father told me that a dog is man'
best friend. Well, friends don't walk out on peopl
because of one bad guess. Friends give people a
second chance, you know!"

I think that's what got him! He blinked again . .
and then he sat down.

Well, he is still sitting and waiting. He is closer t
the garden's edge, but he is still there.

Ogden hugs him a lot, though he doesn't sa
much to him.

You know, I think we're bound to find the righ
name sooner or later. I, myself, am still workin
on the whole thing. He is waiting; I am thinkin
We're both trying.

And, like my mother always says, that's abou
the best anyone can do . . .